S0-AAF-717

Night Boat
to Crete

Penn Mullin

High Noon Books
Novato, California

Cover Design and Interior Illustrations: Nancy Peach

Copyright ©1997, by High Noon Books, 20 Commercial Blvd., Novato, CA 94949-6191. All rights reserved. Printed in the United States of America. No part of this publication may be reproduced, stored in a retrieval system, or transmitted, in any form or by any means, electronic, mechanical photocopying, recording or otherwise, without the prior written permission of the publisher.

International Standard Book Number: 1-57128-056-1

9 8 7 6 5 4 3 2 1 0
2 1 0 9 8 7 6 5 4 3

You'll enjoy all the High Noon Books. Write for
a free full list of titles.

Contents

Corina and Zack are young co-workers at the Park Museum. They are assistants to the museum's director, Claire Long, who sends them to the "four corners of the world" on exciting explorations.

CHAPTER 1

News from Greece!

"Look at this!" Zackary said. He was staring at the computer screen in his office at the Park Museum. "A news item on the Internet about Greece."

"What does it say?" Corina asked.

"Strange bones found on island of Crete. May belong to famous Minotaur!" Zack read.

"The monster who was half-man, half-bull?" Corina asked. "I once read a myth about him. He was supposed to be just make-believe."

"That's what I thought, too," Zack said. "Wouldn't you love to see those bones?"

"Would I! So how do we get the Park Museum to send us to Crete?" Corina asked.

"There must be a way," Zack said. "Wait! I almost forgot. Next year is the big show on Greek art here. What if we could bring back . . ."

"The bones? Get serious, Zack!" Corina laughed, shaking her long shiny black hair.

"No, *pictures* of the bones. Lots of them," Zack said. "I bet Claire would love the idea. And she's head of this museum!"

"Great idea, Zack!" Corina said. "Our museum should have people there where it's all happening!"

2

CHAPTER 2

Hello, Athens!

"Ladies and gentlemen, please fasten your seat belts. We will be landing in Athens in just a few minutes."

"Can you believe it? We're in Greece already!" said Corina. "And we just heard about the Minotaur bones four days ago!"

"I'm so glad Claire liked our plan. We better get lots of good pictures to bring back for the show," Zack said.

"Look! The ocean is so *blue* down there!"

Corina looked out of the plane window. "And all the buildings are so *white*! I can't wait to see Athens!"

"Same here. And we've only got this afternoon to see it. Our boat for Crete leaves at 8," said Zack. "Too bad the airport workers on Crete are on strike. We could fly there in an hour."

"I'm glad we're going on the ferry. We'll get to pass by so many islands," Corina said.

"Greece has 437 of them! I'd like to take a year and visit each one." Zack smiled. "Do you think Claire would pay for that?"

"In your dreams, Zack!" laughed Corina.

The plane gently touched down on the

runway. Then it taxied to a stop at the gate.

Zack stood up and stretched all six feet of his tall thin body. "I feel like I've been turned into a pretzel!" he said.

"Me, too," said Corina. She pulled her laptop computer out from under her seat. "We better e-mail Claire and tell her we're here."

"She's probably afraid we'll get to the beach and forget all about the Minotaur bones," said Zack.

"Now check under your seat. You know how you always forget stuff," Corina laughed.

"Come on, they've opened the doors."

Soon they were getting into their rental car outside the airport.

"Have you got the map?" Corina asked.

"Right here. And let's be careful. These Greek drivers are wild!" Zack said.

"Tell me about it. Were we crazy to rent a car here?" Corina drove slowly through the crowded streets. "Keep watching for the Acropolis. They say you can see it from everywhere in Athens."

"There! I see it – that high hill straight ahead. With the Parthenon on top. Wow, is that beautiful!" Zack whistled.

"There's a parking lot over there. We can leave the car and walk up," Corina said.

Soon they were heading up the path to the top of the Acropolis. "The guidebook says

*"There! I see it – that high hill straight ahead.
With the Parthenon on top. Wow, is that beautiful!"
Zack whistled.*

Akros is the Greek word for 'at the top' and *polis* means 'city.' Makes sense," Zack said. "City at the top."

"Look down at noisy Athens," Corina said. "And up here above it sit these beautiful temples 2500 years old!"

"Look! We're almost on top! The Parthenon is straight ahead. There it is – the real thing!" Zack whispered.

They stood looking up at the huge white marble building with tall pillars all around.

"Can you believe how long this has stood here?" Corina said. "Think of the things it has seen in more than two thousand years!"

"This temple was built as a place for the

statue of the goddess Athena," Zack read. "Corina, I've got an idea. Why don't we just *borrow* the Parthenon for awhile? We could take it back for the museum's Greek show!"

"Oh, yeah!" Corina laughed. "The people of Athens wouldn't mind a bit, I'm sure. Somebody did take a *lot* of the Parthenon home with him once. A man named Lord Elgin took a huge piece of carved marble from it. And now it's in the British Museum instead of here where it belongs."

"I guess they don't let you do that anymore," Zack laughed. "Oh, well, my idea wasn't all bad. I can see the headline: 'Park Museum Brings in Parthenon for Greek Show!'"

"You're too much, Zack," Corina laughed. "Let's see the three other temples up here and then head back down."

"Good idea! We can go down to the *plaka* right below here," said Zack. "Maybe sit at a rooftop cafe and nibble on *baklava*."

"O.K. But first the temples!"

CHAPTER 3

A Stranger Watching

"Well, we made it! But not by much! I think we stopped in every shop in the *plaka*!" Zack laughed. He and Corina stood on the deck of the car ferry for Crete.

Corina smiled. "We really packed a *lot* into one afternoon! And there's so much we didn't have time to see."

The ferry blew its horn and pulled out into the busy harbor of Piraus (Pie-RAY-us). This was the seaport close to Athens.

"The sunset is going to be beautiful," Zack said. "I wish we could have stayed longer in Athens."

"Me, too. But we need to get down to Crete. I have an uneasy feeling about the bones," Corina told him.

Zack looked around the deck at the other passengers. "I wonder how many people are going to Crete because of the bones."

"Only people with special passes can see the bones right now," said Corina. "We're lucky Claire could get us some! The bones are exciting news. But no one is sure yet – did they really belong to the Minotaur?"

"This might be the first time that a monster

in a *myth* turns out to be real," Zack said. "We always think myths are about make-believe gods and animals. But now maybe *not* make-believe. The bones were found *in* the labyrinth itself at the palace. And that's where the Minotaur was said to have lived. It was a maze of hallways that twisted all over the place."

"I think I remember how the myth goes. King Minos of Crete built the labyrinth as a cage for the Minotaur," Corina said. "Every year he made Athens send him 7 boys and 7 girls to feed to the monster."

"They had to run down all those dark halls of the maze," Zack said. "If they chose the wrong way, the Minotaur would eat them!"

"I think I remember how the myth goes. King Minos of Crete built the labyrinth as a cage for the Minotaur. Every year he made Athens send him 7 boys and 7 girls to feed to the monster."

"That's awful! So the people in Athens just kept sending their kids to be killed?"

"No, finally they set up a plan," Zack told her. "They sent Prince Theseus (THIE-see-us) to Crete to kill the Minotaur. He pretended to be one of the 7 boys. The king's daughter Ariadne (air-ee-ODD-nee) fell in love with Theseus. She wanted to save him from the Minotaur. So she gave him a ball of string to unwind in the labyrinth."

"So he could find his way out. Smart lady!" said Corina.

"She also brought him a sword. And that was the end of the Minotaur!" Zack smiled.

"I wonder if the bones are still in the

labyrinth," Corina said.

"Probably. They will fall apart easily because they are so old. The museum people might not want to move them yet," Zack said. "Later they will pick up the whole block of dirt that the bones are in."

"The whole thing is spooky, isn't it? Think of being lost in the labyrinth with the Minotaur chasing you!"

"I'll probably dream about it tonight!" Zack laughed. "We have to sleep sitting up on this ferry, remember? Or sit in our car. All the beds are already taken."

"Look, we're coming to an island," Corina said. She pointed to the white beaches off to the side of the ferry. Everything was covered in the soft pink light of sunset. "I can't believe how many islands Greece has! And how many beaches!"

"It has more miles of coastline than America does!" Zack said. "Not counting Hawaii and Alaska. Greece is a little bigger than our state of Louisiana."

"We've just got to come back here," Corina smiled. "I could be happy in a little shack on one of these islands."

Zack laughed. "So could I!" He looked at his watch. "Hey, it's time for dinner!"

They started walking across the deck. A short dark-haired man slowly followed them. He took his time, pretending to look at the view. But he never stopped watching them.

"Do you see that guy over there?" Corina asked Zack as they got in line for dinner. "The one in the black jacket. He keeps looking at us. There's something creepy about him."

"Yes. He's been watching us ever since we got on the boat," Zack said. "He keeps trying to get near us. As if he wants to hear what we are saying. I'm sure he has us tagged as Americans on our way to see the bones."

"Then we better not talk any more about the Minotaur bones," Corina said. "He might be trying to find out what we know."

"Could be. From now on we'll talk about

something else." Corina and Zack filled their plates and found a table near the window.

"Remember you may have to get up and dance soon!" Corina said. "That's what happens in Greece after dinner. Everybody dances together in a big circle!"

Corina suddenly stopped smiling. The strange dark man had taken a table just behind them.

CHAPTER 4

A Stop in the Night

"Why are we stopping? Are we there?" Zack sat up suddenly. He and Corina had been sleeping on benches in the ferry.

Corina sleepily looked at her watch. "No, we still have another two hours till Crete. I wonder what's happened. There aren't supposed to be any stops on the trip."

Zack stood up. "I'll go try to find out." He started out to the deck in the darkness.

The ferry had stopped at an island. Zack

could see a few people on the dock. But it was too dark to see much else. Then suddenly he saw a person step off the ferry. It was the strange man who had been following them! He walked off into the darkness and was gone.

Where was the man going? Who was he? Zack felt a chill go through his body.

"Why did we stop here?" Zack asked one of the ferry workers on the deck.

But the man just shook his head. He didn't speak English. Zack decided to find the ferry captain. He wanted some answers.

Zack climbed up to the captain's room and knocked on the door. A young crewman opened it. The tall silver-haired captain stood at the window.

"Good morning, sir," said Zack. "Could you please tell me where we are stopped? I thought the ferry went straight to Crete."

"Good morning. Yes, you are right. We always go straight to Crete. No stops," the captain said. "But this morning we had a problem. One of my passengers got bad news in the night. A phone call. His mother is sick. He needed to get off here – at Thora. So we stopped. But we do not like to do this. Now we will be late getting to Crete."

"Do you know the name of the man who got off here?" Zack asked.

"Paros – Stefan Paros. That is what he told

me," the captain said. "Do you know him?"

"No, I was just wondering who he was," Zack answered. "Thank you for your time, sir."

"You are very welcome," the captain said. "I hope you will enjoy your trip!"

Zack went back down to Corina.

"Where did we stop?" Corina whispered.

"At an island called Thora. And our strange friend got off," Zack said. "The captain said the guy's mother was sick on the island. But I wonder if that's so. I have a bad feeling about this."

"He really was creepy," Corina said. "I sure hope that's the last we'll see of him."

"I hope so, too!" Zack said.

CHAPTER 5

Missing!

"Crete! We're finally here!" Zack said. He and Corina stood on the deck with mugs of coffee. The ferry slowly pulled into the harbor of Iraklion (ear-ACK-lee-on).

"This island was a big trading center for the Mediterranean Sea," Corina said. "That fort you see was built in the 1500's. Pirates had to get by that first to attack the harbor."

"How do you know so much? Show off!" Zack laughed.

"What about you and all the stuff you know about myths!" Corina laughed. "Let's go get in our car. We're about to dock."

"Then we can zip right up to the palace where the bones are," Zack said. "But first let's stop at a cafe and get some more of this good Greek coffee!"

"I'll e-mail Claire while you do that. Let her know we're on Crete at last!"

Soon they were parked at a cafe beside the dock. Zack jumped out of the car to go inside. Corina took out her laptop computer. Suddenly there were sirens screaming all around! People were yelling.

"What is it? What's happened?" Corina

called to Zack. He went inside the cafe and came right back out, running.

"The bones are gone! They were stolen this morning!" he said. "I can't believe it."

"What? Aren't there guards at the palace?" Corina asked. "Let's drive up there and see what we can find out." She started the car and they roared up the road.

"Remember you said on the boat that you felt uneasy about the bones?" Zack said. "You sure were right!"

"I hope we can get through all the guards at the palace," Corina said.

"Remember Claire is a friend of Nick Kazan, the man in charge of the bones," Zack said. "That should help us."

The car climbed into the hills through groves of olive and lemon trees. Suddenly they came to a police roadblock!

"Where are you going?" an officer asked.

"To the palace. To see Nick Kazan. We have passes." Corina turned to Zack. "You have them, don't you?"

Zack searched in his wallet. "I know they're in here. I just checked."

The guard looked angry.

"Here they are! I knew I had them," Zack said.

The guard looked at the passes carefully. Then he said, "You may go."

"Thank you," Zack said to the guard. He turned to Corina. "Well, they sure set these roadblocks up fast. Maybe they can catch the crooks before they get off the island."

"Oh, I forgot to e-mail Claire!" Corina said. "I started to back in town. But then things got crazy when we heard the bones were stolen."

"I'm glad *you* forget things, too," Zack laughed. "Makes me feel better!"

"Look at all the police!" Corina said.

She and Zack showed their passes and said only two words – *Nick Kazan*. The police waved their car through the gates.

"That was easy!" Zack laughed. "Just

pretend you know what you're doing. Works every time!"

They left the car and walked towards the palace. "I can't believe we're really here at Knossus (NOSS-us)," Corina whispered. "The oldest part of Greece. And it wasn't even discovered till 1900! Think how it would feel to have been Sir Arthur Evans and find the ruins of this palace!"

"He was amazing. He rebuilt this place the way he felt it would have looked in 1700 B.C. Three and a half thousand years ago! That's when the Minoan (My-NO-en) kings lived here," Zack said.

A guard stepped up to Corina and Zack.

"Mr. Kazan, please," Zack said. The guard pointed to a closed door.

The door opened and a large, worried-looking man stood there. "Yes? What is it? I am very busy right now." He stared at the tall handsome couple in the doorway.

"We work for Claire Burke in America. She told you about us, I think," Corina said.

"Yes! Of course!" The man's face lit up with a smile. "I am Nick Kazan. Welcome to Knossus. Forgive me. This is such a bad time. The bones you came to see – they're gone!"

"Yes, we heard. This is terrible," Corina said. "They were stolen this morning?"

"Very early. Two men," Nick said. "We

think they came by boat. Took the back road up from the beach. They cut wires that sound an alarm in the labyrinth. But a guard heard them and came – too late. He saw them running away. With the bones."

"Who would steal them?" Zack asked. "And why?"

"To sell on the black market. Or maybe they will try to make us pay to get the bones back." Nick shook his gray head sadly.

"Do you have any clues about the robbers?" Corina asked. "Their car?"

"None," said Nick. "Just this." He picked up a black jacket from the table. "There was a ferry ticket in the pocket. The police took it for the fingerprints."

"Wait!" Corina said. "The man on the ferry had a jacket just like that, Zack!"

"You're right! And the ferry ticket – do you know what kind it was, Nick?" Zack asked.

"Athens to Crete. But the ferry just got here an hour ago," Nick said. "The bones were stolen earlier this morning."

"The man in the black jacket got off the ferry early – at Thora," Corina said excitedly. "He could have taken a motorboat here. Had a friend meet him at the beach with a car."

"Then they came up here. I bet he's our man!" Zack said.

Nick was excited. "This is wonderful! You

can tell the police what he looked like. And we'll soon have the fingerprints, too."

"Why do you think this guy was listening to us on the ferry?" Corina asked Zack.

"Maybe he thought we would mention it if the bones had been moved," Zack said. "Because he already had plans to steal them."

"We've closed the whole island," Nick said. "No boats can come in or out. Roadblocks are set up. So I think the men are trapped somewhere nearby, hiding out. Now all we have to do is find them. But Crete is a big island. There are lots of mountains out there. A man could hide for a long time."

CHAPTER 6

The Palace of Knossus

"Did you see the men up close before they got away?" Zack asked the guard who had seen the thieves.

"Not too close. They were running fast. One very big. Thin. The other short, dark. I could not catch them," the guard said sadly.

"Thank you. You have helped us," Corina said. "I'm glad you saw the men. I think this will help the police find them."

Corina and Zack left the guard and walked

"Look at the beautiful dolphins there.
It looks as though they were just painted!"

35

towards the palace. "Let's find the labyrinth and see where the bones were," Zack said.

"Good idea. I really want to see this palace," said Corina. "So much has been rebuilt. Look at the beautiful dolphins there. It looks as though they were just painted!"

"Only a little bit of the dolphin painting was left," Zack read from their guidebook. "A lot of this has been repainted. This was called the 'Queen's Hall' by Evans, who rebuilt it."

Corina said, "We're coming outside now to a big open courtyard. This must have been the center of the palace."

"Look at this!" Zack said. "They even built pipes here to keep the palace from flooding!

They were really modern thinkers."

"And check out this gate," said Corina. "It looks like those are bull horns on top."

"They are!" Zack said. "Bulls were worshiped by the Minoans. I bet those horns up there are over six feet tall!"

Next they walked down into long stone hallways without roofs. One hall led into the next and then turned back into the first one.

"This must be the labyrinth. It just goes on and on! You could go crazy in here!" said Corina. "Even *without* a Minotaur chasing you!"

"I see where the bones were," Zack said. He pointed to where the police were taking pictures of an empty hole in the ground.

"It's really sad," Corina said. "Now we might not ever know if they were really the bones of the Minotaur or not."

"Well, I'm not ready to give up yet," Zack said. "Let's stick around here a few days. I think we might get lucky. Those guys are probably hiding out nearby. They won't dare use the roads. Sooner or later they'll get hungry. They'll have to come out to get food."

"And we think we know what one of them looks like," Corina smiled.

CHAPTER 7

The Long Wait

"Well, they've got to get hungry sometime!" Corina said. "How many days have we sat here watching this market? Maybe someone is taking food to them. They could hide out forever!" She and Zack sat at an outdoor cafe near the palace.

Zack sipped his coffee and watched the people shop at the fruit stands. "Well, this isn't a bad way to spend the day! And we may get lucky if we keep on the lookout here for that guy. Let's not give up yet."

"What happens if we do see him?" Corina asked. "Don't get any ideas about going after him ourselves, Zack!"

"Don't worry. Remember we've got the beeper." Zack tapped his belt. "The police will be all over this place as soon as we hit it."

"At least now we know what his real name is: Stavros Kostas. His fingerprints on the ticket really nailed him," Corina said.

"I was pretty sure he was the guy from the ferry all along. But the picture the Athens police sent – that did it," Zack said. "It was our guy for sure. Boy, he has been in trouble a lot. Always stealing famous works of art."

"I hope he stays far away from *our*

museum," Corina said.

"He'll be behind bars soon I bet. He can't hide forever," said Zack. "Do you want more coffee? It will help us keep awake!"

"Wait!" Corina grabbed Zack's arm. "Look!"

They could see a short dark man standing at the edge of the market. He was looking all around the square. Then he stepped up to one of the food tables.

"It's him! I'm sure it is!" Corina whispered. Zack quickly pushed a button on the beeper and spoke into it.

Suddenly the square was full of police! People screamed. There was the sound of running. Yelling. And then silence. It all happened very fast. Zack and Corina stood at their cafe table and stared at the square.

The police quickly had Stavros in handcuffs. A crowd was growing.

"They got him! Wow, that was fast!" Corina said. "Good thing we had the beeper!"

"You're the one who saw him!" Zack said. "Sharp eyes! Come on. Let's go tell the police what a good job they did!"

Later Corina and Zack were in Nick's office. The Minotaur bones were spread out on the table.

"I'm so glad none of the bones were broken," Nick said. "Why not, I'll never know.

Stavros *ran* with them, hid them in that cave. But now they're safe." Nick smiled at Corina and Zack. "And we have you to thank. It was your idea to watch for Starvos in the market. Claire is lucky to have you. Now, did I hear you are having a Greek show next year?"

"Next spring," Corina said. "And now we have great pictures of the bones for it."

Nick smiled. "I just might come over to your show. I haven't seen Claire in a long time. And I might bring something special from this palace with me. On loan for your show! As long as you two work there, I'm not worried! Everything will be safe!"

"Oh, Nick, wait till Claire hears this

news!" Corina said. "She won't believe it!"

Nick walked them to the gates. "So I'll see you next spring! Maybe by then we will know the truth about the bones. Do they have anything to do with the Minotaur or not? But that is what makes us love this work, isn't it?" He smiled at Corina and Zack.

Corina and Zack started back to the harbor. "I hate to leave this place," Corina said. Do we really have to go back to work on Monday?"

"Yep, the real world calls," laughed Zack. "We better e-mail Claire that we're on our way."

"Already done! And guess how I signed it! Detectives Corina Diaz and Zackary Lane!"